A Book of Bonkers

gorilla ballerina

A Book of Bonkers Animal Poems

Neal Zetter
illustrated by Julian Mosedale

troika

Published by TROIKA

First published 2019

Troika Books Ltd
Well House, Green Lane,
Ardleigh CO7 7PD
www.troikabooks.com

Text copyright © Neal Zetter 2019
Illustrations copyright © Julian Mosedale 2019

A CIP catalogue record for this book
is available from the British Library

ISBN 978-1-912745-05-0

1 3 5 7 9 10 8 6 4 2

Printed in Poland

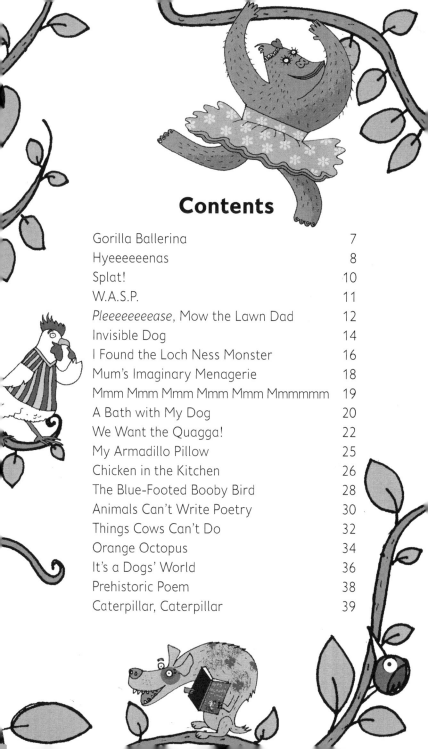

Contents

Gorilla Ballerina

Standing on tiptoe
Putting on a show
Insisting her new hobby is the best way to go
You'd think she'd be rougher, gruffer and meaner
But she's a gorilla ballerina

She just wants the chance
To whirl, twirl and prance
And hoping one day she'll be named the Queen of the Dance
At pirouetting no animal's keener
Check out this gorilla ballerina

In tutu or dress
She'll always impress
Revealing her much softer side, not beating her chest
You'd think she'd be mighty, powerful and stronger
But she's into ballet (and tango and conga)

Gliding 'cross the floor
While the crowds cry "More!"
A maximum ten out of ten is her usual score
You'd think she'd be deadly, a brute and a killer
But she's a ballerina who's a gorilla

Hyeeeeeenas

They're a bit like a wolf
They're a bit like a hound
Have a laugh loud and daft
That's the sound of a clown

Ha ha ha ha
He he he he
Hy hy hy hyeeeeeenas

They have stripes they have spots
Live on African plains
It's their home where they roam
There's no doubt they're deranged

Ha ha ha ha
He he he he
Hy hy hy hyeeeeeenas

Sharpened claws on their paws
On their backs there's a hunch
Always eat lots of meat
For their tea and their lunch

Ha ha ha ha
He he he he
Hy hy hy hyeeeeeenas

What's the joke? No-one knows
But they laugh all the same
First they roar then guffaw
Then they laugh once again

Ha ha ha ha
He he he he
Hy hy hy hyeeeeeenas

Ha ha ha ha
He he he he
Hy hy hy hyeeeeeenas

S POEmS wOt wE
Find SO FunnEE!

Splat!

Tiny spider
- Half-inch long
Did no harm at all

**HORRID HUMAN
SIX FOOT HIGH
SQUASHEDITONTHEWALL!**

W.A.S.P.

I'm a frightful fearful fellow
Dressed in suit of black and yellow
I'm the insect everybody hates to like
I don't care if I alarm you
I'm not bothered if I harm you
Once I've found and fixed you firmly in my sights

See me hover, see me flutter
I'm the nutter in your butter
Forming squishy squashy footprints with my feet
Such a pest and so annoying
I plan soon to be enjoying
That small pot of strawberry jam you've saved for sweet

Horrid humans do not rate me
They will constantly berate me
Much preferring buzzing bees or butterflies
Far too quick forever dodging
All your swiping and your swatting
I'm a terror though a thousandth of your size

When not bugging you for hours
I'm out pollenating flowers
Or off searching for some spiders for my tea
I suggest that you start running
'Cause my sting and I are coming
Call me W and A and S and P!

11

Pleeeeeeeease,
Mow the Lawn Dad

Pleeeeeeeease, mow the lawn Dad
It's like a jungle out there
Full of lemurs, llamas, pythons, piranhas
Raccoons, baboons and grizzly bears

There's a pretty pink porpoise
In love with a tortoise
A huge hippopotamus too
A bobtailed cat
A hog that's too fat
Who escaped from the local zoo

I spy a chinchilla
Chest-beating gorillas
A herd of wild horses stampeding
A sunbathing slug
All kinds of weird bugs
Plus a clever rhinoceros reading

A mountain goat's
Entertaining a stoat
By doing a dance with a fox
While a hoverfly sighs
As she passes by
And sits herself down on an ox

Pleeeeeeeease, mow the lawn Dad
Or at least make a start on the weeding
Salamanders and pandas
Swing from high verandas
And I can hear hyenas screeching

There's a large land snail
Checking his email
A leopard, a leech and a lark
While moles, voles and rats
And four flapping bats
Are venturing out when it's dark

On top of a sheep
(Out cold, fast asleep)
Is a dingo devouring his lunch
A wombat and wolf
Hide under the gorse
While holding their noses near skunks

So *pleeeeeeeease*, mow the lawn Dad
Or this problem we have will not pass
The police will be round
And new animals found
If you don't get rid of that grass!

Invisible Dog

I got an invisible dog for my birthday
It's quite an unusual breed
He goes twice a day for invisible walks
Upon his invisible lead

Together we run round Invisible Park
To chase his invisible ball
I show him off to invisible friends
While at my invisible school

When he has invisible illnesses
He sees the invisible vet
Of all of the animals that she has seen
She says he's the strangest one yet

Invisible dog gives invisible hugs
And lots of invisible licks
He dreams in his basket when sleeping at night
Of fetching invisible sticks

He leaves his invisible doggy dos
Across the invisible ground
I bought big bags of invisible biscuits
To treat my invisible hound

His mouth will emit an invisible bark
When scaring invisible cats
He chews my invisible carpet as well
But I never care about that

The thing is Dad says that it costs far too much
To keep a real dog as a pet
So my imagination made him instead
The most perfect dog you've ever met

I Found the Loch Ness Monster

I found the Loch Ness Monster
Splishing, splashing in my bath
With a Scottish accent
Woolly hat and tartan scarf
Left his chilly Highland home
Swam to London on his own

I found the Loch Ness Monster
I felt shocked, amazed and thrilled
First he stretched then craned his neck
And greeted me "Hi Neal!"
There could be no room for doubt
Nessie nestled in my house

I found the Loch Ness Monster
He gave me a massive fright
Wasn't sure if he was friendly
Or if he would bite
Never met his kind before
Cousin to a dinosaur?

I found the Loch Ness Monster
Born in prehistoric times
Flappy fins, four longish limbs
And spikes right down his spine
He said "I'll not eat a horse
"Feed me haggis with brown sauce"

I found the Loch Ness Monster
So I took him into school
Children wanted photographs
Then cried "He's really cool!"
Teacher shouted "Goodness sake!
"He's that creature from the lake!"

Though this poem's ending here
I think you get the gist
The Loch Ness Monster's not a myth
He definitely exists!

Mum's Imaginary Menagerie

I don't get it
One minute mum says I'm a cheeky MONKEY
Then I'm a greedy PIG
If I eat my veg though she reckons I'll be as strong
    as an OX
And as tall as a GIRAFFE

She moans that I'm like a SNAIL walking to school
And as stubborn as a MULE
I tidied my room on Sunday (yes, tidied my room!)
    and she referred to me as both an eager
    BEAVER and a busy BEE

She tells me not to run down the stairs like a herd
    of ELEPHANTS
But to be as quiet as a MOUSE instead
When mum caught me reading in bed at midnight
    by torchlight she called me a sly FOX

At the dentist I was her brave little LION
So I left there as proud as a PEACOCK
She yells at my sister and me "Stop fighting like
    CAT and DOG!" (though I'm not sure which
    is which)

I think
If I keep listening to mum
Then maybe
I'll grow up to be a wise old OWL like her

Mmm Mmm Mmm
Mmm Mmm Mmmmmm

Q: Why do hummingbirds hum
Unlike any other birds?

A: Although they know the tune
They've forgotten all the words

A Bath with My Dog

Don't think me peculiar
Don't think me odd
But I like to have a bath with my dog

Why go walkies or down the pub
When we can be relaxing in a hot tub?
Just me and Fido
In our own private lido
Not worrying about what others might say
Enjoying the end of a very long day

People warn me "Neal! You'll get in trouble
"Playing with your pet pooch beneath the bubbles"
I reply "Don't be daft"
While soaking in the bath with my dog

He shampoos my hair
I soap his paws
He washes my back
I clean his claws
He rubs my feet
I sponge his tail
He scrubs my ears
I clip his nails

It's great to take a dip
Building our "man's best friend" relationship
He gives a gentle bark
I let out a sigh
There's no room for doggy paddle
Though it's lots of fun to try
When we've done we grab our towels
And wipe each other dry

Human and canine
Are content and fine
With candlelight and white wine
Submerged and entwined
It's what Sunday nights were made for
It's that special time we crave for
I kick the cat out
Lock the front door
When I have a bath
Hear him woof and me laugh
When I have a bath with my dog

We Want the Quagga!

The quagga was a species of zebra, last seen at the end of the 1800s.

We want the quagga!
We want the quagga back
We miss his stripes
Of brown and white
He vanished just like that

We want the quagga!
Why did he disappear?
He seemed such fun
And hurt no-one
He's not been seen in years

We want the quagga!
Where did he wander to?
You won't spot him
In Swaziland
New Zealand or Peru

We want the quagga!
From South African plains
He'd quag and trot
Chew grass a lot
And shake his shaggy mane

We want the quagga!
No longer found in zoos
Although of course
Quite like a horse
A substitute won't do

We want the quagga!
So sadly hunted down
First he was chased
And then erased
Or moved to out of town

We want the quagga!
We love bears, wolves and yaks
Cows, camels, goats
Aardvarks and stoats
But want the quagga back!

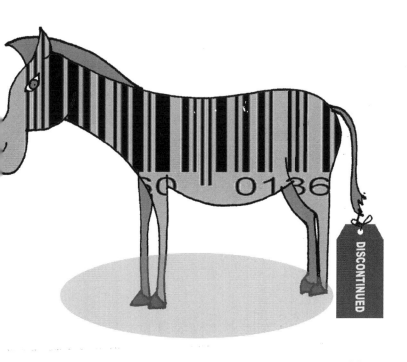

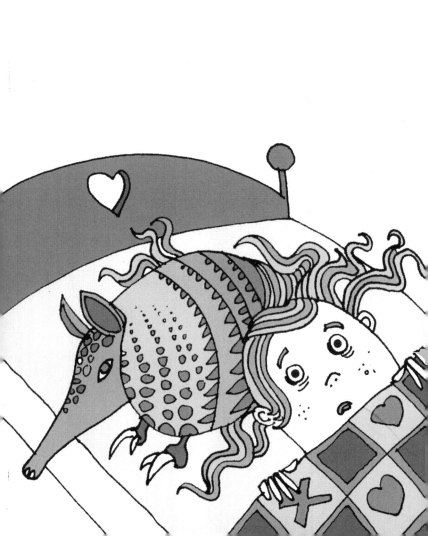

My Armadillo Pillow

My armadillo pillow
Plays havoc with my head
It's scaly, lumpy, bumpy
I'm wanting soft instead

It gives me such a neck ache
I toss and turn all night
What's more it is a creature
That likes to scratch or bite

I know it is a strange thing
Unusual and rare
To rest upon a mammal
Whose claws catch in my hair

A kitten's kinda tiny
A puppy dog is too
A baby bear is bigger
Though can't break out the zoo

A cod could be quite slimy
A lion cub would roar
A monkey's far too funky
A piglet's prone to snore

But we've found a solution
That suits us both real swell
In bed my armadillo
Removes his outer shell

Chicken in the Kitchen

There's a chicken in the kitchen
There's a bat on my hat
There's a bee in my tea
There's a flea on the cat

There's a gibbon in the garage
There's a possum in the park
There's a crab in the lab
There's a moose marooned on Sark

There's a frog on a log
(With a hog and dog)
There's a rhino on the lino
There's a badger in a bog

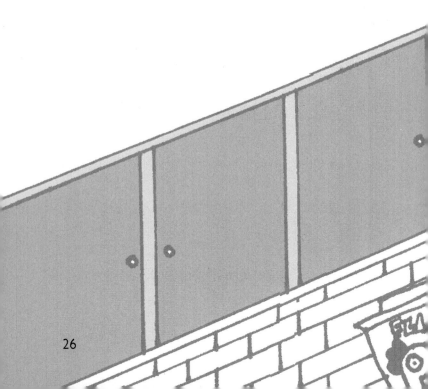

There's a prawn on the lawn
There's a caiman in a cake
There's a hamster in my hair
There's a lizard in the lake

There's a turkey in the toilet
There's a heron in the hall
But where's the dodo gone to
'Cause I can't find him at all?

The Blue-Footed Booby Bird

There is such a bird, native to America and
known for its strange mating dance.

You'll never see a bird like the blue-footed booby
Looking strange enough to live inside a horror
    movie
Beady eyes and pointed beak
He says "booby" we say "freak"

You'll never see a bird that's odder than this
    creature
Took his name and gained his fame from two
    outstanding features
If he could choose now instead
He'd prefer his tootsies red

You'll never see a bird like the blue-footed booby
Tries so hard at acting tough and rough and mean
    and moody
But always the laughing stock
Ought to buy some long white socks

You'll never see a bird like the blue-footed booby
Like a Disney character that's comic and cartoony
Will he ever get a date?
Will he ever find a mate?

You'll never see a bird like the blue-footed booby
Why did Mother Nature make him wacky, weird
    and loopy?
Standing out from any crowd
Other birds all laugh aloud

So ...
If you see a booby bird while visiting the zoo
There's no need to remind him that his feet are
    coloured blue!

Animals Can't Write Poetry

I tried hard to tame them
Teach them and train them
Was offering lessons for free
Though they **woof**, **oink** and **howl**
Roar, **moo** and **miaow**
Animals can't write poetry

I planned to excite them
Thrill and ignite them
But sadly barked up the wrong tree
Though they might perform tricks
Give paws and give licks
Animals can't write poetry

I passed paper and pen to a very keen hen
A thesaurus to a brontosaurus too
It was necessary to lend a rhyming dictionary
To a leopard at London Zoo
I rapped in time with sheep and swine
Read in rhythm to a gibbon I met
But if there's an animal that can write poetry
I still haven't found it yet

I hoped to inspire them
Guide, fuel and fire them
I took them to bookshops with me
Though they **bite**, **chew** and **gnaw**
Scratch, **tear**, **rip** and **claw**
Animals can't write poetry

I wanted to grow them
Sit down and show them
Develop their literacy
Though they might entertain
And have biggish brains
Animals can't write poetry

If you gathered the animal kingdom together
You'd be disappointed because they would never
Never, never
Write poetry

What about me?
William Snakespeare?

Things Cows Can't Do

Cows can't make egg sandwiches
Cows can't play guitar
Cows can't sit a spelling test
Drive buses, trains or cars

Cows cannot throw boomerangs
Cows cannot climb trees
Cows can't run in marathons
Or join a library

Cows can't cut your hair for you
Or wear fancy dress
Cows can't work on building sites
And certainly can't text

Cows cannot fly aeroplanes
Marry or divorce
Cows can't win a game of chess
Or gallop on a horse

Cows cannot send birthday cards
Watch the evening news
And cows can't read this poem aloud
'Cause cows can only
"MOOOOOOOOOOOOOOOOO"!

Orange Octopus

I possess eight feet
Or you might call them hands
I leave wiggly lines
As I crawl across sand
Dress me in shoes and socks
And I'll fumble and fuss
Roaming free
In the sea
I am an orange octopus

Twisting tentacles
Also known as my "limbs"
Are what I choose to use
When I go for a swim
Though I can't ride a bike
Drive a car, coach or bus
Watch me type
Fast as light
I am an orange octopus

I don't own a pen
But I squirt mucky ink
As I make my escape
Quicker than you can blink
The name "cephalopod"
Is what humans gave us
Seven plus one's
More fun
I am an orange octopus

It's a Dogs' World

It's a dogs' world
Different types, breeds, shapes and sizes
Unusual dogs full of surprises
Excited dogs that wag their tails
Extremely strange dogs that miaow
Dangerous dogs whose bites are worse than their bark
Naughty dogs that burst footballs in the park

Dogs that are tall
Dogs that are small
Don't let slobbering dogs lick your face at all
That's totally disgusting and completely uncool

Terriers, Poodles, Spaniels, Alsatians
Labradors, Retrievers, Collies, 101 Dalmatians
A never-ending dog catalogue from so many nations

Dogs out walking
Frightening cats
Some wear coats in winter
But rarely socks or hats
Charcoal black dogs
Chocolate brown dogs
Silver grey dogs
Setters coloured red
Floppy spotted dogs
Silly stripy dogs
Tiny toy dogs
It's unhygienic to let dogs sleep in your bed
Buy them a basket or a kennel instead

Frequently
Dogs must scratch an itchy flea
And drool and dribble while you have your tea
Even though they've just eaten
If you're needing a best friend a dog cannot be beaten

Dogs understand much of what's said
Despite only having two words in their heads
Walkies, dinner
Walkies, dinner
Walkies, dinner
Walkies, dinner
All day long
There's a dog on TV howling along
To his favourite pop song
And a movie star dog in an advert for dog food
Never let dogs grab your slippers as they'll be chewed
    and chewed

Rabbits, hamsters, parrots, gerbils, moggies, horses and
    goldfish are fine
But they cannot compare to a cute canine
Wild dogs
Lost dogs
Guard dogs
Lazy dogs
Superhero dogs
Careful don't tread in doggy do
You'll end up with a smelly shoe

Dogs nervously trembling at the vet
Breaking out in a cold doggy sweat
Sticking by us constantly so we don't forget
That when they say "woof!"
They're telling us they're definitely
The number one
Fun, fun, fun
Most perfect of pets

It's a dogs' world

Prehistoric Poem

Pterodactyl
Pterodactyl
Where is your letter P?
Each time I say your name aloud
It always starts with T
Did you chuck it in the dustbin
Or wash it down the sink?
Perhaps like you it's disappeared
Forever and extinct

Caterpillar, Caterpillar

Caterpillar has something on its head
Hatterpillar, hatterpillar

Caterpillar squashed under my shoe
Flatterpillar, flatterpillar

Caterpillar in flour, egg and water
Batterpillar, batterpillar

Caterpillar wearing a tie
Cravatterpillar, cravatterpillar

Caterpillar with a big round belly
Fatterpillar, fatterpillar

Caterpillar who couldn't care less
Doesn'tmatterpillar, doesn'tmatterpillar

Caterpillar ending this poem (and about time too!)
That'sthatterpillar, that'sthatterpillar

Tarantula Down Your Toilet

I'm the tarantula down your toilet
Your prowler in the pan
I want to bite and frighten you
Whatever way I can
I'll nibble on your bottom
I'll stalk you on the seat
'Cause yes you've guessed
That human flesh
Is what I love to eat

I'm the tarantula down your toilet
I've chosen here as home
Don't linger on the loo too long
While playing with your phone
For when I'm feeling hungry
My fangs will make their mark
You'd better switch the light on
If you enter after dark

I'm the tarantula down your toilet
You'll hear me splash about
Prod me, poke me, push me
But I'm never moving out
I could live in your cupboard
Your kitchen, loft or shed
Yet in this bowl is where I roll
And where I've made my bed

I'm the tarantula down your toilet
Who's causing you dismay
Don't get ideas to calm your fears
By flushing me away
My kingdom is your bathroom
Where I can wander free
So pick a new location
When you have the need to pee

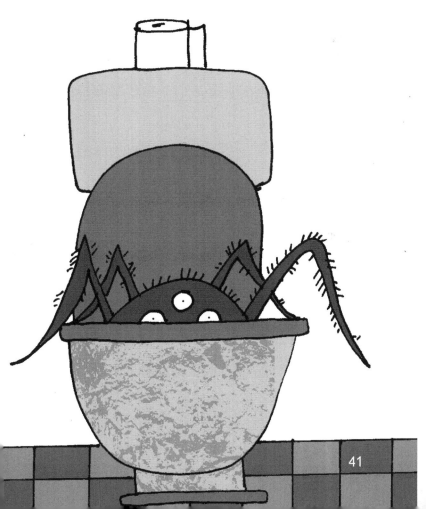

The Yak from Iraq

The Yak from Iraq
Owned an elegant shack
With a huge chimney stack
In a posh cul-de-sac

The Yak from Iraq
Always mooed, never quacked
Had a buddy called Zak
Drove a blue Cadillac

The Yak from Iraq
Wore a pink plastic mac
Plus a pair of silk slacks
Over fur, shaggy black

The Yak from Iraq
Used to sell bric-a-brac
Odds 'n' ends and knick-knacks
That she stored in a sack

The Yak from Iraq
Sitting on the tarmac
Ate a crab for a snack
In a massive flapjack

The Yak from Iraq
Bought her suitcase and packed
Took a train down the track
And she never came back

(That's the last that we saw
Of the Yak from Iraq)

Jellyfish

You're just composed of jelly
With a weird transparent belly
All blubbery and blobby
And your head looks like your body
You sting and spit your poison
Though I still think that you're awesome

Oh deadly creature from the sea
Are you friend or ... anemone?

*(Did you know sea anemones and jellyfish belong to
the same large group of animals called cnidarians?)*

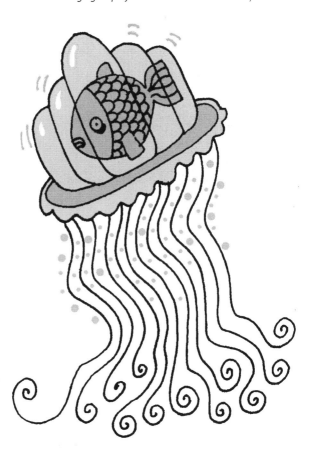

Hide-and-Hippo

You can't hide a hippo in a custard pie
You can't hide a hippo in a cloudless sky
You can't hide a hippo in a pot of glue
You can't hide a hippo in a training shoe
You can't hide a hippo in a garden hedge
You can't hide a hippo on a window ledge

You can't hide a hippo if you paint it green
You can't hide a hippo on a submarine
You can't hide a hippo in a pile of peas
You can't hide a hippo on a high trapeze
'Cause hippos are huge not skinny and sleek
So totally rubbish at hide-and-seek

Hair of the Dog

Why do people put coats
On little Yorkshire Terriers?
If Mother Nature thought them cold
She would have made them hairier

Kangaroo Can

My kangaroo can't bounce
My kangaroo can't hop
He strains to elevate himself
Admits defeat and stops

My kangaroo can't leap
My kangaroo can't bound
I coach, coax and encourage him
Yet he sticks to the ground

My kangaroo can't vault
My kangaroo can't jump
I fitted stabilisers
But he falls flat with a thump

My kangaroo can't bob
My kangaroo can't skip
He'll utterly refuse to use
His brand new pogo stick

So we go for a walk
Or for a gentle trot
If people stare then we don't care
My kangaroo still ROCKS!

Zebra Crossing

Look out!
Zebra crossing!
Creating a fuss
She's bound to be hit by a car, bike or bus
Slowly she strolls
Over the road
Without any care for pedestrian codes

Look out!
Zebra crossing!
Put her on a leash
She's stressing the drivers and giving them grief
Traffic has stopped
Vehicles form queues
How did she escape and break out of the zoo?

Look out!
Zebra crossing!
Wears black and white stripes
Ignoring the law she just does what she likes
Swishing her tail
Shaking her mane
Forgetting she's not on the African plain

Look out!
Zebra crossing!
It's chaos of course
Quite unlike a cow she resembles a horse
"Danger!" I cried
"Watch where you tread!"
"Hey zebra – please use zebra crossings instead!"

49

Elephant in the Room

An "elephant in the room" is an obvious problem or
difficult situation that people do not want to talk about.

Are zebras black with white stripes
Or are they white with black?
Why was that murderer never charged
When we know curiosity killed the cat?

If early birds catch the worms
Why don't worms get there later?
Can an adder also multiply
Without a calculator?

Do all camels have the hump
They seem quite chilled to me?
Fish have no hands
So how'd I get fish fingers for my tea?

It's strange that a wolf in sheep's clothing
With a monkey on his back
Turned into a paper tiger
Once he could smell a rat

Which came first the chicken or the egg?
Neither – dinosaurs of course
Are horses really liquidised
To make horseradish sauce?

We know a man cannot fly
But can a fly man?
Why is it one, three, four and five can't
But toucan?

Would a cheetah be disqualified
When finishing a race?
Why has a hare no hair at all
But has fur in its place?

Are hyenas daft to laugh
When there is nothing funny?
Pull a rabbit from a hat
And you're a clever bunny

You can kill two birds with one stone
Economical, but cruel
While the elephant in the room?
I won't mention it at all

I'm a Skunk

My fur's black and white and fluffy
And my tail is long and bushy
Stink, stank, stunk I'm a skunk

Though I'm sweet I'm also smelly
Bet you won't tickle my belly
Stink, stank, stunk I'm a skunk

I spray poison from my bottom
Yucky, nasty, foul and rotten
Stink, stank, stunk I'm a skunk

As the other creatures fear me
I suggest you don't come near me
Stink, stank, stunk I'm a skunk

When zoo animals throw parties
Then they hardly ever ask me
Stink, stank, stunk I'm a skunk

No-one hugs me it's too risky
And too dangerous to kiss me
Stink, stank, stunk I'm a skunk

If you saw me stood before you
You'd be pleased that I ignored you
Stink, stank, stunk I'm a skunk

I've a scent not nice like roses
Everybody – hold your noses!
Stink, stank, stunk I'm a skunk
I'm a skunk, skunk, skunk, skunk, skunk
PHEW!

Flies

If flies are called "flies"
Then cats should be "prowls"
Monkeys "swings"
With "swoops" the name for owls

Bulls may be "charges"
Horses "gallops" or "trots"
Ducks would be "waddles"
Rabbits and frogs – both "hops"

Let's refer to fish as "swims"
Tigers as "stalks"
Hamsters as "scampers"
And dogs as "walks"
Elephants as "stomps"
Peacocks as "strutters"
Worms as "wiggles"
Butterflies as "flutters"

Bats might be "flits"
Spiders could be "crawls"
But sloths would still be "sloths"
As ...
They ...
Never ...
Move ...
At ...
All ...

How to Spot a Horse

If it won't go wild for hay
Isn't black, brown, white or grey
Never whinnies, never neighs
Then it's probably not a horse

If no rider's on its back
If it doesn't love to hack
Always greets you with a quack
Then it's probably not a horse

If it can't canter or trot
Won't eat carrots (cold or hot)
Sails the oceans in a yacht
Then it's probably not a horse

If it's loathing sugar lumps
Wants to hop instead of jump
If it's grown one or two humps
Then it's probably not a horse

If its neck's without a mane
If it owns a largish brain
Parachutes from aeroplanes
Then it's probably not a horse

BUT
If it won't fit under tables
Is found in a field or stable
Has "HORSE" written on its label
Then of course, of course, of course
It's most definitely, certainly, positively ... a horse!

Don't Pick on Giraffes

Don't pick on giraffes
Don't say they look daft
Don't look at their loooooooooong necks
And poke fun and laugh

Ok they look strange
Peculiar, odd
With heads such a distance away from their bods

I knew one who married a lamppost it's true
I knew one too big to fit into a zoo
I knew one so lanky he'd not seen his toes
And one with a huge scarf he wore in the snow

Ok they look weird
Not what you'd call small
With ears so far up they cannot hear you call

I knew one who lived with his head in the clouds
I knew one who always stood out in a crowd
I knew one who never could find fitting socks
And one even higher than two tower blocks

Giraffes are the tallest beasts you'll ever see
Much taller than you
Much taller than me
They're taller than houses
They're taller than trees
They're taller than all really tall things
So please ...

Don't pick on giraffes
Don't say they look daft
Don't look at their loooooooooong necks
And poke fun and laugh

56

Foul Play

In the Farm Football Cup Final
(Sheep City v United Cows)
The referee was a chicken
So the spectators cried "Fowl!"

Tornado Tortoise

Tornado Tortoise
Always lightning fast
While others plod and ponder
You see him zipping past
Never creeps and never crawls
Never stops and never stalls

Tornado Tortoise
Quickest of his kind
As friends go slow – one mile a year
He leaves them all behind
Eats ten lettuce for his tea
Fantastic velocity

Tornado Tortoise
Such an athlete!
Tiny tortoise trainers
On those tiny tortoise feet
Check out his new running kit
Don't you know he's super fit!

Tornado Tortoise
Won Olympic gold
In the creature hundred metres
Left opponents cold
Has no need to hibernate
Is he using roller skates?

I asked him
"Why are you so swift, Tornado won't you tell?"
He had a think
Then gave a wink
And said ...
"I'm powered by shell!"

The Liger

Is she lion?
is she tiger?
Is she neither?
is she both?
Quite a picture
She's a mixture
She's the feline I like most

An illusion?
A confusion?
Paws and claws
Fur, tail and teeth
Cute and pretty
Giant kitty
She's a most unusual beast

She's a muddle
A befuddle
Bits of this
And bits of that
She's a bungle
In the jungle
She's the craziest of cats

Animal Premiership Table

1. BEARmingham City

2. NEWTcastle Utd

3. Queen's Park REINDEERS

4. West HAMSTER Utd

5. Preston HORSE End

6. MANXchester City

7. Tottenham OCELOTspur

8. Sheffield HENSday

9. BLACKBIRD Rovers

10. STOAT City

11. Aston GORILLA*

12. FuLAMB

13. LiverPOODLE

14. WASPford

15. DerBEE County

16. Brighton & DOVE Albion

And of course:

17. SWANsea City

18. WOLVES

(*Previously known as Aston CHINCHILLA)

Bookworm, Bookworm

Bookworm, bookworm
Head forever found in books
Not moving through the mud
Or dangling from an angler's hook

Impressing the vet
Impressing the zoo
With more knowledge
Than a college
And an infinite IQ

Bookworm, bookworm
Loving fiction, loving fact
Yes this worm has turned
Now eating stories for a snack

Always top of the class
Always top of the tree
A massive brain
The size of Spain
She's off to university

Bookworm, bookworm
It's how she's best described
Adores every shiny cover
And each interesting inside

Wormed her way into a library
Made a bookshop her new home
The cleverest of creatures
The brightest one I've known

Bookworm, bookworm
Books are all she needs
Want to be a brilliant bookworm too?
Then read, read, read
Read, read, read
Read, read, read
And READ!

My Anteater

My anteater's growing thinner
Doesn't like ants for her dinner
Won't eat ants if boiled or roasted
Won't eat ants if baked or toasted

Won't eat ants if briskly fried up
Won't eat ants if slowly dried up
Antburgers won't get a look in
Nor will ant-filled treacle pudding

Won't eat ants if mashed and mangled
Won't eat ants if lightly scrambled
Curried ants are far too spicy
Ant risotto's far too ricey

Won't eat ants with margarine on
Won't eat ants with double cream on
Won't eat ants with jam inside them
Turns her nose up, just won't try them

Won't eat ants in Dijon mustard
Dipped in cold vanilla custard
Won't eat ants in crispy batter
Ketchup won't improve the matter

Won't eat ants with salt and pepper
Cream cheese, Stilton, Brie or feta
Won't eat ants in hot fajitas
She's an anti-ant anteater

I'm an Electric Eel

I'm an electric eel
Delivering shocks
An electric eel
Blowing off your socks

An electric eel
Giving you a jolt
An electric eel
Can you feel my volts?

I hang out in river beds
Touch me you might end up dead

I'm an electric eel
Even scaring sharks
An electric eel
Glowing in the dark

An electric eel
Don't eat me with chips
An electric eel
I will burn your lips

Slimy, smooth and slippery
Full of electricity

I'm an electric eel
See me splash and swim
An electric eel
Long and sleek and slim

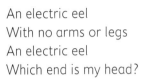

An electric eel
With no arms or legs
An electric eel
Which end is my head?

Run on mains or battery
Looks like someone's flattened me

I'm an electric eel
Such a powerful chap
An electric eel
With a zap, zap ...
ZZZZZZZZZZZZAP!

Bats! Bats! Bats!

With special thanks to the letter B.

British, Bulgarian, Brazilian bats
Bosnian, Bermudan, Bolivian bats
Bright brainy bats
Bulging-belly bats
Big-bottomed bats
Blue bats buzzing
Brown bats bawling
Black bats braying
Beige bats beeping
Blonde bats burping

Bats! Bats! Bats!

Brutish bats biting bears
Bullying bats bothering bees
Bickering bats bugging birds
Baby bats being born
Brad, Brian, Billy bat
Beth, Brie, Becky bat
Beware!
Batman's buddies – bold brave bats
Battling, breaking, busting, bruising, beating
Baddie biker bats

Bats! Bats! Bats!

Bouncing bats
Boing! Boing! Boing!
Builder bats
Bish! Bash! Bosh!
Boxing bats
Bam! Bang! Bump!
Boring bed batzzzzzzzzzzzzzzzzz
Baking bread bats
Buttering baguettes
Burning bagels
Buying baps
But borrowing brioche
Babbling bats blathering
Blah! Blah! Blah!
Before bellowing **"BOO!"**
Bats! *Bats!* *Bats!*

Bossy, brash, busy, boogieing, breakdancing
Boisterous, breathtaking, bodacious, brilliant, bonnie
Bonkers, barmy, barking, bananas, batty

BATS! BATS! BATS!

(Bye-bye)

The Acrostic Animal is ...

An amazing, astounding

Curious, cute, clever

Rare, ruby-red

Oblong or oval

Shy, shimmering, shiny

Timid, tranquil, tiny

Intelligent, interesting, inquisitive

Chubby, cheerful, creature

Jellyphant

No common elephant
I'm a jellyphant
Composed of gelatine
My herd all say
"He isn't grey
"More luminous lime green"

I never stomp
I never stamp
I wobble on my feet
Most elephants
Are rough and tough
I'm yummy, soft and sweet

I'll entertain you
At the zoo
So brilliant to behold
Not jungle born
But crafted from
A massive jelly mould

I don't squirt water
From my trunk
Just cold custard or cream
Part animal
Is what I am
And part confectionery

I squash and squidge
Sleep in a fridge
To keep my body firm
I'm a giant
Jolly jellyphant
The strangest pachyderm

I'm Not Too Old
to Own a Teddy Bear

I may be too old to learn my ABC
I may be too old to watch kids' TV
I may be too old to eat in a high chair
But I'm not too old to own a teddy bear

I may be too old to swim in paddling pools
I may be too old to go to primary school
I may be too old to have a full head of hair
But I'm not too old to own a teddy bear

I may be too old to ride roller skates
I may be too old for candles on my cake
I may be too old for dodgems at the fair
But I'm not too old to own a teddy bear

I may be too old to play a game of snap
I may be too old to try to rap, rap, rap
Sucking my thumb's now extremely rare
But I'm not too old to own a teddy bear

I may be too old to blow bubble gum
I may be too old for a smack on the bum
Alone in the dark I'm too old to be scared
But I'm not too old to own a teddy bear

I may be too old for fish fingers with chips
I may be too old for buying sherbet dips
You can say I look stupid but I just don't care
'Cause I'm not too old to own a teddy bear

Two-in-One Animals

ElephANT
WallaBEE
EaGULL
MeerCAT

HippopotaMOUSE*
CaiMAN
MonGOOSE
WomBAT

(*Optional alternative: HippopotaMOOSE)

CaiMAN

WomBAT

HedgeHOG

Don't Eat the Animals

*This poem first appeared in "Yuck and Yum (A Feast of Funny Food Poems)"
so if you like it, buy the book (also published by Troika).*

Don't boil a bat
Don't bake a snake
Don't microwave a millipede
Don't cook koala cake

Don't grill a gorilla
Don't gnaw on a macaw
Never fry a fruit fly
Don't even have it raw

Don't coddle a cockroach
Don't fricassee a frog
Don't poach piranhas, ants, iguanas
Tapirs and hogs

Don't chomp on a chicken
Don't chew a kangaroo
Munching mandrills for a snack
Is not the thing to do

Don't steam a sea bass
Don't barbecue a bear
Don't serve a salamander
Medium rare

Don't pickle a penguin
Don't try terrapins on toast
Don't liquidise lynx for smoothie drinks
Don't make a rhino roast

Don't sauté a salmon
Don't catch a crab to crunch
Because the zoo will disappear
If you eat it for lunch

Animal Scramble

Chickens miaow
Marmosets moo
Anteaters bark
Crocodiles coo

Jaguars chirp
Elephants cluck
Wallabies quack
Convinced that they're ducks

Octopuses oink
Tortoises howl
Wildebeests baa
Walruses growl

Scorpions squawk
Polar bears squeak
Since a witch and wizard
Visited the zoo last week

Meet the Gorilla Guys

Neal Zetter is an award-winning London-based comedy performance poet, author and entertainer with a huge following in schools. Since 1989 he has used his talents to develop literacy, confidence, self-expression and creativity in 3–103 year olds. He performs in schools almost every day and has also worked in more unusual places including comedy clubs, theatres, music venues, a League 2 football match, the Royal Festival Hall, a funeral and even at his own wedding. This book is his eighth for Troika. Neal's first memorable encounter with an animal was when his grandad gave him a teddy bear which he still possesses, 57 years on.
More on Neal: cccpworkshops.co.uk

Julian Mosedale has never won an award for anything but is confident that his latest drawings for Mr Zetter will finally see him recognised as the misrepresented and underappreciated genius that he truly is. ("He is you know!" – actual quote from Mrs Mosedale.) He has illustrated literally *brazillians* of books and they are all over that interweb thing so have a look! He has been a teacher and ruined all the boring subjects for the kids of North London. He has recently decided to write his own wonky poems and generally makes a nuisance of himself in the publishing world. Julian Mosedale loves to draw animals or anything really (but not bicycles or fingers – they're too tricky). He actually made friends with a gorilla while he was studying them at a zoo for his college degree. He won't bore you with that story now but ask him about it next time you meet him...
More on Julian: www.julianmosedale.co.uk

Two more SUPER poetry books from Troika

ISBN 978-1-909991-45-3

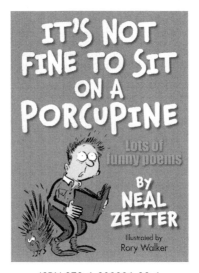

ISBN 978-1-909991-28-6